#10

SOCCER 'CATS

Kick It!

Matt Christopher®

Text by Stephanie Peters

Illustrated by Daniel Vasconcellos

D0967509

LITTLE, BROWN AND COMPANY

New York ॐ An AOL Time Warner Company

Library of Congress Cataloging-in-Publication Data

Peters, Stephanie.
  Kick it! / Matt Christopher ; text by Stephanie Peters ; illustrated by Daniel Vasconcellos.
    p. cm. — (Soccer 'cats ; #10)
  Summary: After Alan accidentally kicks his teammate Eddie during a game, he not only has problems kicking but also has to endure teasing by another fullback.
  ISBN 0-316-73808-5   ISBN 13: 978-0-316-73808-8
  [1. Soccer — Fiction. 2. Friendship — Fiction. 3. Guilt — Fiction. 4. Interpersonal relations — Fiction.] I. Vasconcellos, Daniel, ill. II. Title.
PZ7.P441833 Ch 2003
[Fic] — dc21   2002035925

Printed in the United States of America

Soccer 'Cats Team Roster

Lou Barnes	*Striker*
Jerry Dinh	*Striker*
Stookie Norris	*Striker*
Dewey London	*Halfback*
Bundy Neel	*Halfback*
Amanda Caler	*Halfback*
Brant Davis	*Fullback*
Lisa Gaddy	*Fullback*
Ted Gaddy	*Fullback*
Alan Minter	*Fullback*
Bucky Pinter	*Goalie*

Subs:

Jason Shearer

Dale Tuget

Roy Boswick

Edith "Eddie" Sweeny

Chapter 1

Alan Minter wiped the sweat off his nose and put his glasses back in place. All the action was down at the other end of the soccer field at the moment. But he knew that that could change very swiftly. One hard kick by a Panther could send the ball into 'Cat territory. As one of the Soccer 'Cats fullbacks, it was his job to help defend the goal. He didn't want to be caught off guard.

Sure enough, a minute later the Panthers were on the attack. The strikers passed the ball back and forth, dodging around the 'Cat halfbacks. The halfbacks gave chase, but it wasn't enough. The Panthers were deep into 'Cat territory. It was up to the fullbacks now.

Alan bounced on his feet, ready to move. He kept careful watch on the Panther with the ball. She was dribbling quickly down the side of the field farthest from Alan and seemed determined to bring the ball right up to the goal.

Then Alan caught a movement out of the corner of his eye. He turned his head. Another Panther was running down the other sideline, waving his hand in the air!

She's going to pass to him! Alan thought. His legs were already carrying him to the space between the two Panthers. A moment later, he'd intercepted the pass.

With a strong kick, he booted the ball down the sideline to where Lou Barnes, a 'Cat striker, was waiting. Lou took off, dribbling madly.

"Great steal! Nice kick!"

Alan slapped hands with his fellow full-back Edith "Eddie" Sweeny.

"Man, it's hot out here today." Eddie's fiery red hair and face were damp with perspiration. "Glad we don't have to do as much running as those strikers."

Alan nodded. As he did, his glasses slipped down his sweaty nose again. He took them off and used the hem of his T-shirt to wipe his nose.

"Here they come! Heads up!"

The shout took Alan by surprise. He looked up. Without his glasses on, the attacking Panthers were just a blur of movement. But even he could see they were coming fast.

He ran to his position, fumbling to put his glasses back on as he did. To his horror, he dropped them.

He had two choices: play without them and hope they didn't get stepped on, or search around for them — and hope he didn't get stepped on!

He chose to play. And it was a good thing he did because the Panther offense was attacking on his side of the field.

Alan threw himself headlong into the fray. He made out the shape of the ball and stabbed his foot at it. The ball squirted free.

Alan was the first one to reach it. He planted his left foot on the ground and slashed his right leg forward with all his might. As he did, another player moved in front of him.

He tried to stop his kick, but it was too late! His foot met bone — and he heard a scream of pain followed by the shriek of the referee's whistle.

Chapter 2

Who is it? Who did I kick?" Alan asked frantically. "Is he—or she—okay? Where are my glasses?"

Someone handed him his glasses. Miraculously, they had not been broken. Alan put them on and stared at the sight in front of him.

Eddie lay on the grass. She looked pale. Coach Bradley was kneeling beside her, holding an ice pack to her chin. Blood seeped out from under the pack.

"Oh, man, oh, man," Alan moaned. "Is she okay?"

Coach Bradley pulled his cell phone from his pocket. "I'm not sure, Alan. I'm going to call for an ambulance, just in case." He dialed 911, told the operator the situation, and hung up. Then he and the referee carefully lifted Eddie and carried her to the sidelines.

Minutes later, the ambulance drove up with its lights flashing. By that time, Eddie's mother had arrived. She climbed into the back of the ambulance with Eddie. The doors closed, and the ambulance disappeared down the street.

Alan couldn't believe it. He'd kicked his friend in the face and sent her to the hospital!

He felt a hand slap him on the back.

"Nice going, Minter," drawled Brant Davis. Brant played fullback for the 'Cats, too. "Or maybe I should call you Slugger instead? Get it? Slug her?" He laughed.

Alan stared at Brant. "I don't think that's very funny," he said. "Eddie could be really hurt!"

Brant rolled his eyes. "Oh, please. You have a strong kick, but it's not *that* strong! She'll be fine."

Before Alan could reply, the referee blew his whistle. The game was going to start again.

Coach Bradley laid a hand on Alan's shoulder. "Are you okay to play?" he asked. "I can sub Jason in for you if you'd like."

Alan shook his head. "No, I—I'm fine," he said. Jason Shearer had missed the last week of practice because his family had been on vacation. Alan thought he might be a little rusty. Besides, there were only a few minutes left in the game.

Coach Bradley looked at him carefully, then nodded for him to take his position.

"That a boy, Slugger," Brant called as Alan jogged onto the field.

"Brant, stop calling me that or else!" Alan hissed.

Brant held up his hands, pretending to be scared. "Or else what? Or else you'll—

you'll—*kick me?*" His laughter was drowned out by the shrill of the referee's whistle.

Darn that Brant! Alan fumed. He tried to put him out of his mind. But when he did, the image of Eddie's bloody chin popped in. Alan squeezed his eyes shut.

What if she's not okay? The thought tormented him for the rest of the game. So did Brant, who called him Slugger every chance he got.

Alan had never been so happy for a game to end in his life. As soon as the ref blew his whistle, Alan took off for home. He didn't even bother to see who'd won.

Chapter 3

Alan burst in the door of his kitchen. He found the telephone book and looked up Eddie's number. But when he dialed the number, all he got was the answering machine. With a sigh, he left his name and number and his reason for calling. He wished he knew where the ambulance had taken her.

Mrs. Minter came into the kitchen to find Alan slumped at the table. "Goodness, what's wrong?"

Alan told her what had happened.

Mrs. Minter picked up the phone. "She's

probably at Mercy Emergency." She dialed a number, waited, then spoke to the person who answered. She jotted down some information on a piece of paper, then hung up.

"Eddie's going to be fine," she reported. "She needed a few stitches in her chin, that's all. And she has one whopper of a headache."

"Stitches?" Alan didn't like the sound of that.

His mother ruffled his hair. "Tell you what. Why don't you take a quick shower, then we'll go to the mall and see if we can find something to bring Eddie to cheer her up. How's that sound?"

"Could we go see her tonight?" Alan wanted to know.

Mrs. Minter shook her head. "Let's save the visit for tomorrow, after she's had a good night's sleep, okay?"

Alan nodded, then headed to the bathroom for a shower. When he emerged, he found a

snack waiting for him. He ate it quickly, wanting to get to the mall as soon as possible.

Ten minutes later, he and his mother were wandering through the aisles of a toy store.

"Do you think she'd like a stuffed animal?" Mrs. Minter asked. She held up a soft dog and made its tail wag. Alan gave a weak smile, but shook his head.

"I think she'd like a game better," he said. They moved on to the game aisle.

"How about Chinese checkers?" Mrs. Minter pulled a box from the shelf. Alan examined it.

The game board was shaped like a star. Each point was a different color and held marbles of the same color in little holes. The marbles winked in the light. Alan thought the game looked pretty, but he wondered if it was fun to play.

Mrs. Minter explained the game. "The object is to be the first one to get your marbles across the board and into another star point. You can only move one marble one space at a time, although you can jump over an opponent's marble to get to an open spot."

"Do you capture the marbles, like in regular checkers?"

His mother shook her head. "No. But if you're clever, you can block your opponent and keep her from being able to move where she wants to go," she answered. "So, what do you think?"

Alan nodded. "Let's get it," he said. He hoped Eddie would like it.

Chapter 4

When they got home from the mall, Alan wrapped the game. The next morning, he carried it to Eddie's house. Eddie herself answered the door.

Alan tried not to stare. Eddie's chin was covered with thick gauze held in place by white tape. Some of the gauze had little red spots on it. Alan realized the spots were blood. He felt a little queasy.

Eddie, on the other hand, seemed like her usual self. "It hurts a little bit when I smile or laugh," she said. "But the doctor says I'll be fine. If there's a scar, it'll be tough to see."

She led Alan into the kitchen. "What's that?" she asked, eyeing the present.

Alan finally found his tongue. "It's for you."

Eddie tore open the package. "Chinese checkers! Cool!" she exclaimed. Then she winced and put her hand to her chin.

"Are you okay?" Alan asked anxiously.

"Yeah, yeah," Eddie grumbled. "Sometimes the tape pulls my skin, that's all." She sat down and pulled the lid off the game. "So, want to play?"

Alan sat across from her. "If you're sure you're not too tired, or — "

Eddie waved her hand. "I told you, I'm fine! I'm going to be the green marbles," she said. "You be red."

Alan was soon so absorbed in the game that he forgot about Eddie's injury. The two played Chinese checkers for the rest of the morning. Only when the clock struck eleven did he remember he had to go home for lunch.

"Thanks for playing with me," Eddie said, closing up the board. "Come again tomorrow?"

"Sure," Alan replied. He felt much better. Eddie really did seem to be all right.

He left her house whistling a tune. As he rounded a corner, he bumped into Brant — and his good mood vanished.

"Whoa, Slugger. Don't kick me, I'll get out of your way!"

"Very funny," Alan said, trying to move past him.

Brant moved with him. "So, what brings you to my street?" he wanted to know. Then he snapped his fingers. "Wait a minute. Eddie lives over there, doesn't she? What were you doing, returning to the scene of the crime or something?" He laughed again.

Alan rolled his eyes and kept walking. *That Brant really burns me up!* he thought angrily.

*   *   *

The next day, Alan headed for Eddie's house again. Along the way, he passed an empty lot filled with wildflowers. He knew it was nice to bring sick or injured people flowers, so he picked a bunch to bring to Eddie. To his dismay, he ran into Brant again just as he was leaving the lot.

"Slugger!" Brant cried. He looked at the flowers and raised his eyebrows. "Are those for me?"

Alan tried to push by him, but Brant caught his sleeve. "Hold on. Are you bringing those to Eddie?"

Alan pulled free and hurried away. But he wasn't fast enough to keep from hearing Brant call out, "Alan's got a girlfriend! Alan's got a girlfriend!"

Chapter 5

Alan didn't see Brant on his way home from Eddie's that day. That was fine with him. He knew he'd see him at the soccer field the next day, when the 'Cats played the Torpedoes.

Maybe he'll be tired of teasing me by then, Alan thought. But somehow, he doubted it.

He was right. The minute he arrived at the field the next afternoon, Brant sidled over to him.

"Hey, Slugger, looks like your girlfriend came to cheer you on." He pointed to the stands. Eddie was sitting there. Her bulky gauze had been replaced by a smaller bandage. When she saw Alan and Brant looking at her, she waved.

"Aww, isn't that sweet?" Brant cooed. Then he laughed and walked away, leaving Alan burning with embarrassment.

The 'Cats and the Torpedoes warmed up, then took their positions on the field. The ref blew his whistle, and the game began.

The Torpedoes had won the coin toss, so they had the ball first. The center striker nudged it to his left wing. The wing quickly passed it to the other wing. The right wing took off down the field, dribbling carefully.

Amanda tried to stop him. The Torpedo dodged around her, then passed back to the center. Bundy did his best to intercept the pass, but he missed. Suddenly, the Torpedo offense was heading right for the goal!

Ted Gaddy and Brant went after the player with the ball. Lisa Gaddy and Alan hung back, keeping an eye on the other two forwards. If the center passed the ball off, they would be ready to steal it.

Ted finally freed the ball. He booted it to the side, but the kick wasn't strong enough to get it out from in front of the goal. The Torpedo nearest to Alan rushed to get it. But Alan was a step closer. If he could get off a quick, solid kick, he could send the ball down to where the 'Cat halfbacks were waiting.

As the Torpedo bore down on him, he pulled his foot back. But at that second, the memory of what it had felt like when his foot had struck Eddie's chin popped into his head.

Swish! He missed the ball completely!

Alan spun around just in time to see the Torpedo slamming the ball past Bucky Pinter and into the net. Torpedoes 1, 'Cats 0.

Alan was dumbfounded. The Torpedoes had scored on their very first play of the

game—and it was all his fault for missing the ball.

"Put it out of your mind, Alan, and get into position," called Bucky from the goal. "It's our turn to put one between their posts!"

"Yeah, shake it off, Alan," Ted echoed.

Alan nodded. He felt bad about the goal and was determined not to mess up again.

Yet less than five minutes later, he flubbed another kick. Once again, he was racing a Torpedo to the ball. And once again, just as he was about to give the ball a hard boot, he remembered the accident.

This time he managed to kick the ball—but his kick was so weak the ball only dribbled forward a few feet! The Torpedo looked surprised, but quickly recovered. She swung her leg forward and booted the ball right into the net. Torpedoes 2, 'Cats 0.

If Alan had felt bad before, now he felt miserable. This time no one told him to shake it off. In fact, no one said anything—except Brant.

"Hey, Slugger, stop daydreaming about your girlfriend and keep your mind on the game!"

Chapter 6

The rest of the first half was a disaster for Alan. He messed up kick after kick. Finally, he just stopped going for the ball at all.

Coach Bradley had no choice but to sub Jason in for him at the start of the second half. Alan didn't blame him. He would have done the same thing.

Partway through the second half, the coach sat down beside him.

"Everything okay, Alan?" he asked.

Alan sighed. "I don't know what was wrong

with me today, coach," he admitted. "I just couldn't seem to kick the ball, that's all."

The coach was quiet for a moment, then he said, "Alan, kicking Eddie was just a freak accident. Anybody could have done it." He glanced at the stands. Alan could hear Eddie screaming encouragement to her teammates. "And she seems perfectly fine, don't you think?"

Alan nodded.

"So I think you owe it to yourself and your team to forgive yourself and put what happened out of your head. If you do, I'll bet you get your kick back."

"I'll try," Alan promised.

"That's all I can ask for," the coach said. "Now why don't you sub in for Ted? He looks like he needs a rest."

Alan shot the coach a grateful look. Then he checked in at the scorer's table and ran onto the field when the ref gave him the go-ahead.

He had every intention of following the

coach's advice. And he did try his best to—but no matter what he did, his kicks were always off. It came as no surprise when Ted returned to the game, sending Alan back to the bench.

There were still five minutes left to the game, but Alan had had enough. When he was sure no one was looking, he slipped off the bench and hurried away from the field.

That night, Alan was picking at his dinner when the phone rang. It was Bucky.

"Hey, Alan, where'd you get to today? I looked for you after the game, but didn't see you anywhere!"

"I—I just came home, that's all," Alan said, knowing he was only telling half the truth.

"Yeah, well, listen. I know you were having trouble with your kicks today,"—Alan winced—"and I thought you might like me to help you work on them."

Alan was surprised. He wondered if the

coach had put Bucky up to this. Then he realized he didn't care. Bucky was a good friend. He was offering to help because he wanted to, not because someone had told him to.

"That'd be great, Bucky," Alan said. "What did you have in mind?"

"Come over tomorrow morning, and we'll get to work," he said. "See you then!"

Alan hung up. He felt better than he had all day.

Chapter 7

Bucky was rummaging around in his garage when Alan biked into his driveway the next morning.

"Hey, Alan, go on into the backyard!" he called. "I'll be right there!"

A moment later, Bucky came out with what looked like a big lump of plastic and a bicycle pump. Alan watched with curiosity as Bucky inserted the tip of the pump into the plastic and started pumping.

Soon, the plastic blob had changed into a tall blow-up clown. Bucky gave the clown a push. It toppled over to one side, then sprang back up straight again.

Bucky tossed the pump aside.

"Who's the clown?" Alan joked.

Bucky grinned. "Kicking practice." He grabbed a soccer ball and moved to the center of the yard. "I'm going to kick to you. You stop the ball and kick it as hard as you can at the clown. If you knock him to the ground, you've hit him hard enough. Okay?"

Alan nodded. Bucky kicked the ball toward him.

Alan ran forward and stopped the ball. He tried to kick it, but just like in the game, it only dribbled forward a few feet, then stopped. Bucky retrieved it.

"Try again!" Bucky yelled. He fired the ball to Alan.

This time, Alan missed completely. He started to groan, then saw that Bucky was looking at him with a puzzled expression.

"What?"

"Alan," Bucky said slowly, "do you know that you close your eyes just as you're about to kick the ball?"

Alan stared at Bucky, dumbfounded. "I *what?*"

"I could be wrong, but I'm pretty sure you close your eyes just before you kick the ball," Bucky repeated. He squeezed his eyes shut to demonstrate.

"That's ridiculous," Alan protested. "Why would I do that?"

Bucky shrugged. "Search me." The boys were silent for a few minutes, puzzling over Bucky's discovery. Suddenly, Bucky snapped his fingers.

"Alan, remember when Amanda was hit in the face with the soccer ball and got a bloody nose?"

Alan nodded. "Yeah, it was gross. So?"

"She couldn't head the ball for days after that because she was afraid of getting hit again!" Bucky reminded him.

Alan suddenly understood what Bucky was trying to tell him. "Do you think I started closing my eyes because of the accident?" The image of Eddie lying on the ground with blood on her chin popped into his head again.

"You're doing it right now!" exclaimed Bucky.

To his amazement, Alan realized Bucky was right. He'd squeezed his eyes shut when he thought about Eddie.

"Well, now that we know *why* you do it," Bucky said, "we have to get you to *stop* doing it!"

"And how are we going to do that?" Alan wanted to know.

Bucky bounced the soccer ball off his knee and caught it. "We're going to keep doing the drill," he said. "Only every time you're about to kick, I'm going to yell to you to keep your eyes open. Okay?"

Alan got up. "Okay, I'm ready if you are."

His first tries at knocking the clown over

failed. He either missed the ball or gave only weak kicks. But with Bucky's encouragement, he soon started to kick harder and on target.

"Yes!" he cried happily the first time the clown flopped over. After that, he hit the clown more than he missed.

They practiced for another hour, then opened the plug on the clown and took turns stomping on him until he was deflated.

"Thanks again, Bucky," Alan said.

"No sweat," Bucky answered. "Just don't forget what you learned before our next game!"

Chapter 8

Alan's kicking was put to the test the next day. The coach had called for a practice.

"I'm happy to report that Eddie is back and ready to play again," Coach Bradley said after everyone had arrived.

Eddie grinned as the team applauded. "Thanks, everyone," she said. "Your cards and everything really cheered me up last week."

"Did she like your flowers?" whispered Brant to Alan. Alan glowered at him.

"In honor of Eddie's return, I thought we'd

work on defense today," the coach continued. He separated them into teams of five — two offense, two defense, and a goalkeeper.

Alan was paired up with Brant. They were defending against Lou Barnes and Jerry Dinh. Bucky was their goalkeeper. They were the third team in line.

The coach tossed the first group a ball. "Offense, I want to see you working those passes. Defense, try double-teaming the player with the ball or marking the offense man-to-man. Whenever you get the ball, kick it as hard and as fast as you can to clear it from in front of the goal. Ready? Begin!"

Stookie Norris dribbled forward a few feet, then passed the ball to Amanda Caler. Ted and Bundy Neel swarmed her. Amanda immediately passed back to Stookie Norris. Stookie tried to dribble forward again, but Ted stole the ball and kicked it out of reach.

The coach blew his whistle. "Good work.

Next group!" he called. Eddie and Lisa took their positions against Dewey London and Roy Boswick.

"Going to cheer for your girlfriend?" Brant grinned wickedly at Alan. Alan just glowered at him.

Dewey and Roy fought to reach the goal against Eddie and Lisa. Eddie had a look of determination on her face. With a quick jab of her foot, she captured the ball from Dewey. Then she booted it clear.

"Yes!" she said, pumping her fist in the air.

Brant leaned in to Alan. "C'mon, aren't you going to give her a hug or a kiss or something?"

Alan opened his mouth to retort, but he didn't have the chance. The coach was calling their group.

Brant smiled sweetly. "It's our turn. See if you can't kick the ball better today than you did against the Torpedoes, okay?"

Furious, Alan took his position. *I'll show you*, he said to himself. He tensed as Lou and Jerry started to dribble and pass. As they neared, he repeated the same words over and over to himself.

Keep your eyes open, keep your eyes open, keep your eyes open.

Suddenly he saw his chance. He zoomed forward, stole the ball from Lou, and pulled it to one side with a quick move of his right foot. Now all he had to do was boot it clear.

He took a quick deep breath, pulled his leg back—and connected with the ball for the hardest kick he could ever remember making!

The ball soared down the sideline, finally bouncing to a stop well past the midfield line.

"Whoa!"

"Holy cow!"

"Nice kick!"

His teammates all congratulated him. Bucky

gave him a big smile. Alan was thrilled. He'd licked his problem!

"Not bad," Brant said as they got back in line. "Of course," he continued, "this is just a drill. Let's hope you can do the same thing during a game."

Chapter 9

Alan's heart sank. Much as he hated to admit it, Brant was right. What if he couldn't kick during a game?

Well, I can't worry about that now, he said to himself. *I'll just have to try my best, that's all.* He hoped he could follow his own advice.

Practice ended fifteen minutes later. Bucky and Alan started walking home together. Eddie caught up to them.

"Hey, Alan, I was wondering if you'd like to come over and play some more Chinese checkers? Bucky, you can come, too, if you want."

The boys agreed. On their way to Eddie's house, Brant passed them on his bicycle.

"Uh-oh, is someone trying to steal your girl, Slugger?" Brant called over his shoulder. Laughing, he pedaled away, leaving Eddie and Bucky puzzled and Alan blushing behind him.

"That Brant can be such a pain," Eddie said. "Know what he calls me sometimes? Big Red." She shook her red hair.

"Really?" said Bucky. "I never heard him call you that before!"

"He's always careful only to say it when no one else can hear him," Eddie said, frowning. "Bet he never makes fun of you guys!"

"Huh! Guess again!" Alan blurted out.

Eddie and Bucky turned to him, surprised.

"He—he started calling me Slugger the day I kicked you," he admitted. He hesitated, then told them about Brant calling Eddie his girlfriend. To his relief, Eddie just rolled her eyes.

"Good grief, you were just being nice! And I would have been bored to death if you hadn't visited me," she said. "Now, is that all, or did he say something else that bugged you?"

"Just one other thing," Alan said. "He—he said he wondered if I'd be able to kick during a game." He told Eddie about the troubles he'd been having with kicking and how Bucky had helped him with the problem.

Eddie laughed. "Boy, kicking me has caused you more trouble than it caused me! But I think I've got an idea that will help you solve both problems." She grinned. "What if every time you go to kick the ball, you pretend it's Brant? You can get out your anger at him—and you'll be sure to kick with extra power!"

The boys laughed, too. Alan wasn't sure he'd follow Eddie's suggestion—as mad as he was at Brant, the idea of pretending to kick him didn't seem right—but it sure was good to know others understood how he felt.

Chapter 10

Two days later, Alan, Bucky, and Eddie were sitting on the bench together, waiting for their teammates to show up for the game against the Tadpoles. One by one, the others appeared. Brant was one of the last to arrive.

After some warm-up drills, the teams took their positions.

Alan was determined to play his best. Eddie was starting the game because Lisa was home sick. Alan glanced over at her. He could see a look of determination on her face as well.

"Try to pay attention to the game, not your girlfriend," Brant whispered to Alan just before the ref blew his whistle.

Alan gritted his teeth. Then he caught Eddie giving him a look that said "forget about him." Alan grinned and nodded to her.

Alan wasn't too worried about playing against the Tadpoles. Their offense wasn't usually that good, so most of the play occurred down at the other end of the field.

Today, however, the Tadpoles took the 'Cats by surprise. They started off strong, sending the ball back and forth across the field with short, crisp passes. Before the 'Cats could recover, the ball was near the 'Cat goal!

Eddie and Alan rushed to double-team the player with the ball, just as they had practiced earlier in the week. Alan freed it with his foot. He knew he had only a moment to clear it from the goal before the Tadpole tried to take it back from him.

He pulled his leg back. The split second before he was about to kick, he remembered Eddie's suggestion. He couldn't help it—as his leg swung forward, he imagined the ball was Brant.

Wham! The ball left his foot and flew down the sideline. It was traveling so fast, one Tadpole ducked to get out of its way. Lou Barnes scooped it up on his foot and started off for the Tadpole goal.

After that kick, Alan didn't look back. Although he didn't imagine the ball was Brant again, he played the best game of his life, clearing the ball with solid kicks and dogging the offense so much that they started making mistakes.

Even Brant was impressed. After the game, he admitted he'd never seen him play better. "That first kick of yours in particular was amazing," he said. "You must have been showing off for your girlfriend!"

Alan glanced at Eddie and Bucky. "Actually, I just pretended the ball was something that makes me mad," he said innocently. "And, boy, did it feel good to kick it!"

"By the way, Brant, you played a good game, too," Eddie said. She slapped him on the back.

"Gee, thanks, Big Red," Brant said. "Well, see you guys later." He turned and walked away.

Eddie nudged Alan and pointed at Brant's back. Alan looked and doubled over with laughter.

When Eddie had slapped Brant's back, she'd left something behind — a sign that read "Kick Me!"

SOCCER 'CATS

CPSIA information can be obtained
at www.ICGtesting.com
Printed in the USA
LVOW04s0806210516
489305LV00010B/17/P